The New Creatures

MORDICAI GERSTEIN

HarperCollins*Publishers*

Library of Congress Cataloging-in-Publication Data

Gerstein, Mordicai.
    The new creatures / Mordicai Gerstein.
        p.   cm.
    Summary: An old man tells his grandchildren about a sheep dog
named Herman who, during the days when dogs and cats ruled the
world, discovered the first humans.
    ISBN 0-06-022164-X. — ISBN 0-06-022167-4 (lib. bdg.)
    [1. Dogs—Fiction.   2. Cats—Fiction.]   I. Title.
    PZ7.G325He   1991   90-4128
    [E]—dc20   CIP
                                                                                  AC

The illustrations in this book were done with
pen and ink, watercolor, and colored pencil on heavyweight vellum.

For all the
cats and dogs,
ducks and foxes,
and for that
wonderful painter,
Canaletto

Herman, the old sheepdog, stood by the door and made strange mumbling noises.

"Herman wants his walk," the old man said to the children.

"But it's sleeting outside," said the boy.

"And I'm doing my history homework," said the girl.

"I'm afraid Herman comes first," their grandfather replied.

Herman loved his walk, even in the wind and sleet. He
pulled the children through icy puddles and explored every inch
of the street as if he'd never seen it before.

He was soaked by the time they got home. The boy and girl had to dry and brush him while he dozed by the fire.

"What do *you* want, Ishtar?" the girl asked the cat, who rubbed against her and mewed.

"It's time for her supper," said the old man. "Tuna and poached eggs, that's all she'll eat."

"Dogs and cats are nice," said the boy, "but it seems all we do is wait on them!"

"Sometimes I wish they'd take care of themselves," said his sister, "like when they lived in the wild."

"Oh, dogs and cats were always too smart to live in the wild." The old man chuckled. "Herman and Ishtar told me that long ago."

"They don't really talk to you, do they?" asked the girl.

"They talk to everyone," replied her grandfather. "Most people just don't understand them."

"What do they say?" asked the boy.

"Yes, tell us," asked the girl.

Sleet rattled the windows, and the old man looked deep into the fire. The children looked too, and waited for their grandfather to continue. Ishtar purred and smiled, and Herman sighed through his nose and seemed to mumble something.

"Herman has told me," their grandfather said at last, "that long long ago, the dogs and cats ruled the world. They had their own countries, with magnificent dog and cat cities.

"In those days they weren't so furry, and they walked on their hind legs and wore rich clothing decorated with rare jewels.

"Their only faults were greediness and laziness. They always wanted more, and tried to get other animals to do their work for them.

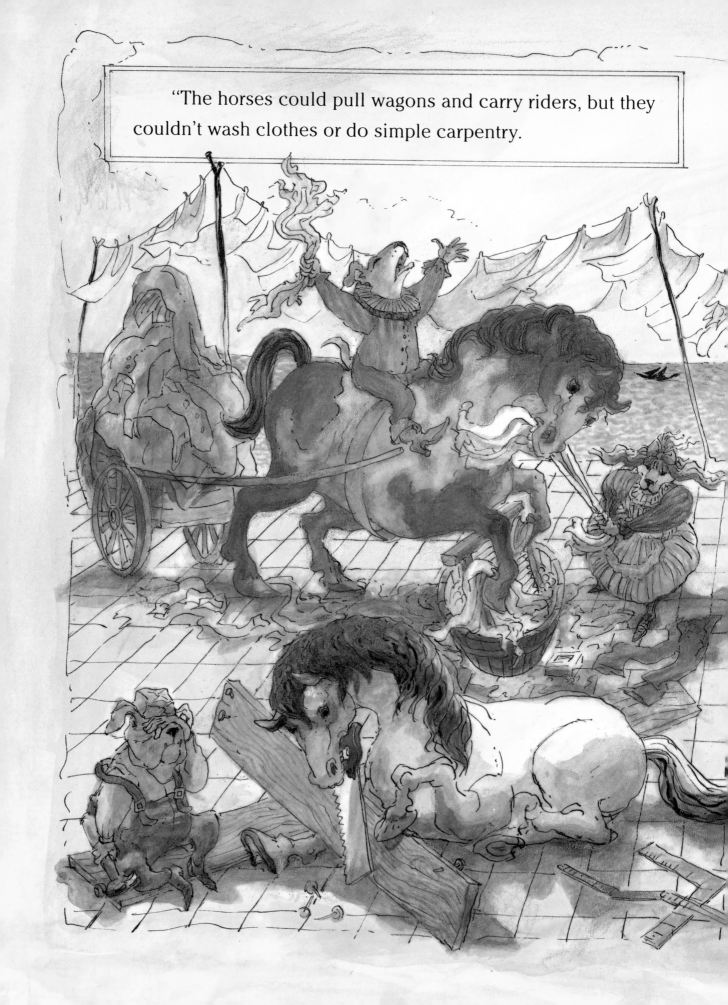

"The horses could pull wagons and carry riders, but they couldn't wash clothes or do simple carpentry.

"The cows licked dishes clean, but couldn't bake a cake or churn butter.

"They tried to teach sheep to spin and weave their own wool, but it was hopeless.

"The foxes were too smart to work, and the ducks wouldn't do anything at all.

"So the dogs and cats squabbled constantly about who would do what. After a while, their streets and houses became a terrible mess.

"It was during this period, called the Age of the Terrible Mess, that a dog named Herman decided he'd had enough. He went off into the wilds to see what else there was in the world. My Herman was named after him.

"He was the first explorer. He went through jungles and over mountains till he found a hidden valley. In the valley he found a new creature.

"It walked on all fours and had no fur; it covered itself with leaves. It didn't seem too smart, but it was friendly. Herman found that if he gave it food, it would do whatever he wanted. Unlike dogs and cats, who were finicky, this new creature loved anything edible.

"Herman brought a small herd of the creatures back to civilization.

"First they were put in zoos and circuses. The cats and dogs taught them tricks.

"Then they became popular pets. Kittens and puppies liked to play with the new creatures' babies.

"Soon they were put to work. The dogs taught them to herd ducks, sheep, and pigs.

"The cats taught them to pull carriages and whip cream.

"Dogs taught them to stand on their hind legs and hunt foxes. Cats taught them weaving and cleanliness.

"After a while, the dogs and cats had nothing to do but play or just lie around and give orders. They didn't even have to stand up. They began to walk on all fours.

"Since they didn't have to go to work, the dogs and cats didn't bother to get dressed. They got furrier while the new creatures learned to dress themselves.

"Finally, the dogs and cats didn't even have to give orders.

They taught the new creatures to train themselves, and to give each other orders. Everything was taken care of."

"What were the new creatures called?" asked the boy as he poked the fire.

"They were called Herman's Beings, after the dog who discovered them. Today, of course, we're called humans."

The boy burst into laughter. "Grandpa!" He giggled. "That's the silliest story you've ever told us."

"We humans have always ruled the world," said his sister. "We learned that in school."

Grandpa laughed, and Herman made a sound very like a chuckle. Then he rolled over on his back, which meant he wanted his belly rubbed. The children rubbed it.

Ishtar purred and pushed her head under Grandpa's hand, which meant she wanted her head scratched. Grandpa scratched it.

The fire was just embers and everything was quiet.

"Grandpa…" said the boy after a minute or two, "we humans really do rule the world…don't we?"

His grandpa didn't answer at first. Then he began to snore.
Ishtar meowed something in cat language, then she purred.
Herman made his chuckling sound and sighed.
Then they were all snoring softly.
Together.